With love to my mother,
Bettie Kessimakis
—D.S.

For Megpie
—V.A.

Mother Goose's
PAJAMA
PARTY

Danna Smith ★ Illustrated by Virginia Allyn

Doubleday Books for Young Readers

STAR LIGHT, STAR BRIGHT,
COME TO STORY TIME TONIGHT.
BRING YOUR FRIENDS
AND DON'T BE LATE.
MEET AT MY HOUSE –
HALF PAST EIGHT.

– MOTHER GOOSE

The moon was first to see the note.
She showed the cow what Mother wrote.

The cow told Dish, and Dish told Spoon.
Spoon told Cat, who fiddled a tune.

Cat whispered to a boy named John
with one shoe off and one shoe on.

Jack-a-Dandy filled a sack
and slung his treats across his back.

Wee Willie Winkie spread the word
and Georgie Porgie overheard.

He told Bo-Peep with one quick kiss,
then shared it with another Miss,
who left behind her curds and whey
and ran to pick a bright bouquet.

Mary, Mary picked one too,
while Betty tried to find her shoe.

Nimble Jack, so spry and quick,
led them with his candlestick.

They came upon a crooked house,
a crooked man and crooked mouse.

Then all together, single file,
they walked the final crooked mile.

Right on time at half past eight,
they marched through Mother Goose's gate.

They dressed in jammies old and new.
Mother Goose wore PJ's too.
Handy spandy Jack-a-Dandy
shared his cake and sugar candy.

They gathered in the reading nook
with Mother Goose's famous book.

She read of those who sat beside her,
Dish and Spoon and Muffet's spider.

She read of those who were not there,
like Simple Simon at the fair.

She read of ships and seas they roam.
She read until Peep's sheep came home.

With happy hearts and bellies stuffed,
yawns were yawned and pillows fluffed.

She kissed each little sleepyhead
and tucked them soundly into bed.

Then Mother Goose blew out the light.
"Sleep, my children.
Sweet dreams."

TWINKLE, TWINKLE, LITTLE STAR

Twinkle, twinkle, little star.
How I wonder what you are,
up above the world so high,
like a diamond in the sky.
Twinkle, twinkle, little star.
How I wonder what you are!

STAR LIGHT, STAR BRIGHT

Star light, star bright,
first star I see tonight,
I wish I may, I wish I might
have the wish I wish tonight.

THE CAT AND THE FIDDLE

Hey diddle diddle,
the cat and the fiddle,
the cow jumped over the moon.
The little dog laughed
to see such sport,
and the dish ran away with the spoon.

DIDDLE DIDDLE DUMPLING

Diddle diddle dumpling, my son John
went to bed with his trousers on,
one shoe off and one shoe on.
Diddle diddle dumpling, my son John.

HANDY SPANDY JACK-A-DANDY

Handy spandy Jack-a-Dandy
loves plum cake and sugar candy.
He bought some at the grocer's shop
and out he came, hop, hop, hop.

WEE WILLIE WINKIE

Wee Willie Winkie runs through the town,
upstairs and downstairs in his nightgown,
tapping at the window, crying at the lock,
"Are all the children in their bed? It's past ten o'clock."

LITTLE BO-PEEP

Little Bo-Peep has lost her sheep
and doesn't know where to find them.
Leave them alone and they'll come home,
wagging their tails behind them.

GEORGIE PORGIE

Georgie Porgie, puddin' and pie,
kissed the girls and made them cry.
When the boys came out to play,
Georgie Porgie ran away.

LITTLE MISS MUFFET

Little Miss Muffet
sat on a tuffet,
eating her curds and whey.
Along came a spider,
who sat down beside her
and frightened Miss Muffet away.

MARY, MARY, QUITE CONTRARY

Mary, Mary, quite contrary,
how does your garden grow?
With silver bells and cockleshells
and pretty maids all in a row.

BETTY BLUE

Little Betty Blue
lost her holiday shoe.
What can little Betty do?
Give her another to match the other
and then she may walk in two.

THERE WAS A CROOKED MAN

There was a crooked man and he walked a crooked mile.
He found a crooked sixpence upon a crooked stile.
He bought a crooked cat, which caught a crooked mouse,
and they all lived together in a little crooked house.

JACK BE NIMBLE

Jack be nimble,
Jack be quick,
Jack jump over
the candlestick.

SIMPLE SIMON

Simple Simon met a pieman
going to the fair.
Said Simple Simon to the pieman,
"Let me taste your ware."

Said the pieman to Simple Simon,
"Show me first your penny."
Said Simple Simon to the pieman,
"Indeed, I have not any."

Simple Simon went a-fishing
for to catch a whale.
But all the water he could find
was in his mother's pail!

Simple Simon went to look
if plums grew on a thistle.
He pricked his fingers very much,
which made poor Simon whistle.

He went to catch a dicky bird,
and thought he could not fail
because he had a little salt
to put upon its tail.

He went for water with a sieve
but soon it ran all through.
And now poor Simple Simon
bids you all adieu.

I SAW A SHIP A-SAILING

I saw a ship a-sailing,
a-sailing on the sea.
And, oh, but it was laden
with pretty things for thee.
There were comfits in the cabin
and apples in the hold.
The sails were made of silver,
and the masts were made of gold.